EMMA YARLETT

KING
LION

WALKER BOOKS
AND SUBSIDIARIES
LONDON • BOSTON • SYDNEY • AUCKLAND

The LION was KING.
King of a kingdom where
everyone was HAPPY...
"Everyone except me,"
sighed the King.

Every day he looked down
on his kingdom and felt more
and more ALONE.

Until one day,
he had an idea.
"I need a FRIEND!"
said the king.

He knew exactly
what to do.

But everyone just

ran

away.

He tried everything!
Waving his PAWs...

Flashing a SMILE...

Cracking a JOKE...

But nobody understood and
the king felt DREADFUL.
"All I want is a friend,"
sighed the king.

And so he tried one last time. He climbed to a place where EVERYONE would see him.

And from the top of the tallest tower,
he asked, "PLEASE, will ANYBODY
be my FRIEND?"
But all they saw were his
DANGEROUS CLAWS.
And all they
   heard were his
DEAFENING ROARS.
And all they
   feared were his
DRIPPING JAWS.

And all of them said,
"The KING is DREADFUL."

So the KINGDOM hid
from their DREADFUL king.
And the lonely King Lion
became WILD with sadness.
So every night he ROARED his
SORROW into the DARK.

But nobody understood.

Until one day, a small girl
was playing all alone when—

SHE SAW HIM.

She saw his DANGEROUS claws.
And she heard his DEAFENING roars.
And she feared his DRIPPING jaws.

But...

she thought perhaps she understood.

So that night, she made a
DREADFULLY brave plan.

Who is his friend?

king Me

us?

I need a friend too!

What could I say?

Hello

Hey

Hi

is lion sad

where do I find him?

Turn that frown upside down →

what's so terrible?

TERRIBLE

KING LION

HIDE FROM THE BEAST

is he just misunderstood?

What if he's just trying to say hello?

Do lions make good friends?

The next day, as the
lonely king Lion prowled
his empty kingdom...

she was waiting
for him.

And so the LION flashed his DANGEROUS claws...

But so did she!

So he roared his DEAFENING roars...

But so did she!

So then he opened his dripping jaws...

And she did exactly what she had come to do.

"HELLO,"
said the little girl.
"LET'S BE FRIENDS."

Because she understood.
And she understood what it was
to NEED a FRIEND.

And soon, the king
understood what it was
to BE a FRIEND.

And from that moment on, the girl and the king were always dreadfully...

happy.

FOR BEA,
the brave and kind little girl who inspired this book.

First published 2023 by Walker Books Ltd, 87 Vauxhall Walk, London SE11 5HJ

2 4 6 8 10 9 7 5 3 1

© 2023 Emma Yarlett

The right of Emma Yarlett to be identified as author of this work has been asserted in accordance with the Copyright, Designs and Patents Act 1988

This book has been handlettered

Printed in China

British Library Cataloguing in Publication Data: a catalogue record for this book is available from the British Library

ISBN 978-1-5295-0159-9

www.walker.co.uk